Snow White and the Seven Dwarfs

Illustrated by Dorothea King

Brimax Books Newmarket England

Once there was a little
princess called Snow White.
Her stepmother was
a wicked Queen. The Queen
was very beautiful. Every day
she looked into her magic
mirror and said,
"Mirror, mirror on the wall,
Who is the fairest of them all?"
Every day the mirror would reply,
"You, oh Queen, are the
fairest in all the land."

One day the Queen asked,
"Mirror, mirror on the wall,
Who is the fairest of them all?"
And the mirror replied,
"You, oh Queen, are very fair,
But Snow White is the fairest
in all the land."
Instead of seeing her own
face in the mirror the Queen
saw the face of Snow White.
She was very angry.

The Queen sent for her huntsman.
"Take Snow White into the
forest and kill her," she said.
The huntsman loved Snow White.
"I cannot kill you," he said,
taking Snow White into the forest.
"But you cannot go home.
You must stay in the forest."
The huntsman returned to the
palace alone. He told the
Queen he had killed Snow White.

Snow White wandered alone through the dark forest. She came to a little house. "Perhaps the people who live here will help me," she said. She knocked at the door. There was no reply, so she peeped inside. It was a very untidy house. Everything in it was very small. There was seven of everything – seven chairs, seven spoons, seven mugs and seven plates.

Snow White was so hungry she ate some bread from the table. Then she said, "I will tidy up for the people who live here." She swept and dusted, cleaned and polished. She had plenty of helpers. Then, because she was tired she lay on one of the seven beds and fell fast asleep.

The cottage was lived in by seven dwarfs. They worked in a mine on the far side of the forest.

When they got home they found Snow White asleep. Snow White woke up with a start.

"Who . . . who are you?" she asked. "This is our house," said the dwarfs. "Do not be afraid, we will not hurt you, but tell us what you are doing here."

Snow White told the dwarfs what had happened.

"You can stay here and we will look after you," said the dwarfs. Snow White and the dwarfs lived happily together. But the dwarfs were afraid the wicked Queen would come looking for Snow White. They told her not to open the door to anyone. They were right to be worried.

The Queen asked her mirror,
"Mirror, mirror on the wall,
Who is the fairest of them all?"
The mirror replied,
"You, oh Queen, are very fair,
But Snow White who lives in
the forest with the little men,
is the fairest in all the land."
The Queen was very angry.
"I will kill Snow White
myself," she said.

The Queen dressed herself as a pedlar. She filled a basket with apples, then went into the forest. She waited until the dwarfs had gone to the mine, then she knocked at the door of the little house. "I have nothing to fear from a pedlar," said Snow White. And she opened the door.

"Good day, child," said the Queen.
"Would you like one of my apples?"
"Oh, yes please . . ." said
Snow White.
The Queen gave Snow White
the reddest apple in the basket.
It was a very special apple.
The Queen had put a spell on it.
"Take a bite . . ." said
the Queen.

Snow White took one bite
from the apple and fell to
the ground.
"Ha! Ha!" laughed the Queen.
"Snow White is dead. Now
I am the fairest in all the land."
When the dwarfs came home,
they found Snow White
lying on the ground. The
apple was lying beside her.
"The wicked Queen has been
here," they said sadly.
"Snow White is dead."

The dwarfs built a special bed for Snow White in the forest. The animals kept watch around her.

One day a Prince came riding by and saw Snow White lying there. "Please let me take her home," he said.

As the Prince lifted Snow White onto his horse she opened her eyes. The piece of magic apple had fallen from her mouth.

"Snow White is alive!"
shouted the dwarfs.
"Hoorah! Hoorah!"
Once more the Queen asked,
"Mirror, mirror on the wall,
Who is the fairest of them all?"
The mirror replied,
"You, oh Queen are very fair,
But Snow White, the Prince's
bride is the fairest in all
the land."
The Queen was so angry, she
flew into a rage and died.
Snow White was safe at last.